The author would like to thank Dr Gerald Legg
of the Booth Museum of Natural History, Brighton,
for his help and advice

VIKING

Published by the Penguin Group
Penguin Books Ltd, 27 Wrights Lane, London W8 5TZ, England
Penguin Books USA Inc., 375 Hudson Street, New York, New York 10014, USA
Penguin Books Australia Ltd, Ringwood, Victoria, Australia
Penguin Books Canada Ltd, 10 Alcorn Avenue, Toronto, Ontario, Canada M4V 3B2
Penguin Books (NZ) Ltd, 182-190 Wairau Road, Auckland 10, New Zealand

Penguin Books Ltd, Registered Offices: Harmondsworth, Middlesex, England

First published 1993
1 3 5 7 9 10 8 6 4 2
First Edition

Text copyright © Theresa Radcliffe, 1993
Illustrations copyright © John Butler, 1993

Filmset in Bembo

Printed and bound in Singapore through Imago Productions (F.E.) Pte Ltd

Library of Congress Catalog Card Number: 92.85417

A CIP catalogue record for this book is available from the British Library

ISBN 0-670-83852-7

SHADOW THE DEER

Theresa Radcliffe
Illustrated by John Butler

VIKING

It was early summer in the forest.

The leaves on the old oak tree had opened at last.

Beyond the oak tree was a thicket of brambles and some young hazel trees and here, hidden in a hollow under the bramble bushes, lay Shadow the deer.

She lay quietly, waiting for evening to come.

Then it would be safe to leave the shelter of the brambles to look for food.

Her sleeping fawn lay near her.

He was only three days old.

At last the light in the forest began to fade and evening came.

Shadow got up quietly. She was hungry and thirsty.

It was time to leave her new fawn and look for food.

She pressed him down gently with her nose and he

looked back at her.

He knew he had to lie very still now.

Shadow left the shelter
of the thicket and made her way through the
long undergrowth towards the old oak tree at the edge of the clearing.
She stood still for a moment – looking and listening for danger.
But everywhere was quiet. She moved across the clearing,
pulling at the long green grass.

It began to rain softly.

Shadow lifted her head and looked back for a moment to where her

fawn lay sleeping.

She wanted to go to him, but she knew she had to go on.

She was thirsty and she had to find water.

She slipped quickly and silently through the forest, towards the lake.

Shadow reached the lake and bent down to drink.

A bat swooped low over her head and startled her.

She drank quickly, anxious to get back to her fawn.

Meanwhile, on the far side of the forest, some
fox cubs had come out of their earth and were
playing together in the new bracken.
Two of the cubs had found an old rabbit bone.
They growled and fought over it.
Redflank, their mother, watched them.
She knew they were hungry.

Redflank left the cubs, scrambled down the
steep slope to a small stream and ran across
a moss-covered log.
She stopped for a moment, sniffing the air,
then hurried on into the darkest part of the forest.

She was heading for the bramble thicket by the old oak tree.

There the hunting would be good.

She would catch the voles who made their homes in the

long undergrowth.

Redflank reached the thicket and crept forward into the brambles.

She crouched down, head to one side, listening for voles, ready to pounce.

And then she saw him!

There in front of her, only a few feet away, lay the sleeping fawn.

Redflank trembled, her nose quivered.

She smelled the fawn's warm smell and thought of her hungry cubs.

The fawn slept on.

Redflank crept closer.

At this moment, Shadow was hurrying back towards the thicket. She heard a pheasant's harsh call of alarm.

She knew something was wrong.

Her fawn was in some kind of danger.

He needed her, she had to get back to him.

Faster and faster she ran through the forest.

She reached the edge of the clearing just as Redflank was about to attack.

Shadow sprang across the clearing towards her fawn –

she would let nothing harm him!

Redflank turned to face Shadow, snarling, furious that she might lose her meal.

Shadow charged.

She struck the vixen with her front legs.

Redflank shrank back, but did not run.

Shadow turned and charged once more, jumping over her,

hitting her again and again with her hard hooves.

This time Redflank knew she was beaten.

Hungry and defeated, she ran back through

the forest to her own cubs.

Shadow went to her fawn.

He was awake now and waiting for her.

He stood up on his wobbly legs and nuzzled against her.

Shadow licked his head.

The danger was over.

Darkness fell and the screech of an owl filled the forest.

Shadow would not leave her fawn again that night.